فرشتگان آلفی

ALFIE'S ANGELS

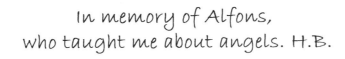

In memory of Alfons,
who taught me about angels. H.B.

For Mum, Dad and Daniel,
for your support and encouragement. S.G.

First published 2003 by Mantra
5 Alexandra Grove, London N12 8NU
www.mantralingua.com

Text copyright © 2003 Henriette Barkow
Illustrations copyright © 2003 Sarah Garson

British Library Cataloguing in Publication Data:
a catalogue record for this book is available
from the British Library.

فرشتگان آلفی

Alfie's Angels

Henriette Barkow

Sarah Garson

Farsi translation by Parisima Ahmadi-Ziabari

mantra

آلفی میخواست یک فرشته باشد.
او آنها را در کتابهایش دیده بود.

Alfie wanted to be an angel.
He'd seen them in his books.

او آنها را در رویاهایش دیده بود.

He'd seen them in his dreams.

Angels have wings and angels can fly.
Alfie wanted wings so he could fly to
school on time.

فرشتگان بال دارند و فرشتگان می‌توانند پرواز کنند. آلفی می‌خواست بال داشته باشد تا بتواند بموقع به مدرسه اش پرواز کند.

Angels can dance, and sing in beautiful voices.
Alfie wanted to sing so that he could be in the choir.

فرشتگان می توانند برقصند، و با صدای زیبایی آواز بخوانند.
آلفی میخواست آواز بخواند تا بتواند در دستهٔ کُر باشد.

فرشتگان می توانند سریع‌تر از آنکه با چشم د یده شوند حرکت کنند.

Angels can move faster than the eye can see.

آلفی میخواست تندتر حرکت کند تا بتواند
گُل‌های بیشتری‌به دروازه بزند.

Alfie wanted to move faster so
that he could score more goals.

فرشتگان به‌همهٔ شکل ها هستند...

Angels come in all shapes...

...همهٔ اندازه‌ها،

...and sizes,

و آنها قادرند کارهای شگفت انگیزی انجام دهند.

and they can do the most amazing things.

آلفی میخواست یک فرشته باشد.

Alfie wanted to be an angel.

او آنها را در کتابهایش دیده بود.
او آنها را در رویا هایش دیده بود.

He'd seen them in his books.
He'd seen them in his dreams.

حالا سالی یکبار بچّه‌ها می‌توانند فرشته شوند.
آموزگاران آنها را انتخاب می‌کنند.
اولیاء آنها را لباس می‌پوشند.
همهٔ مدرسه آنها را تماشا می‌کنند.

Now once a year children can be angels.
The teachers choose them.
The parents dress them.
The whole school watches them.

Alfie's teacher always chose the girls.

آموزگار آلفی همیشه دخترها را انتخاب می‌کند.

زیباترین دختران. دخترانی که موی خیلی بلند دارند.
دخترانی که چشمهای درشت و خنده ایی دلنشین دارند.

The prettiest girls. The girls with the longest hair.
The girls with the biggest eyes, and the sweetest smiles.

But Alfie wanted to be an angel.
He'd seen them in his books.
He'd seen them in his dreams.

امّا آلفی میخواست یک فرشته باشد.
او آنها را در کتابهایش دیده بود.
او آنها را در رویایش دیده بود.

وقتی که آموزگار پرسید ”چه کسی می خواهد فرشته شود؟“
آلفی دستش را بالا برد.

When the teacher asked, "Who wants to
be an angel?"
Alfie put up his hand.

دختران خندیدند. پسرها زیر لبی و با تمسخر خندیدند.

The girls laughed. The boys sniggered.

آموزگار به او خیره شد. آموزگار فکر کرد و گفت،
”آلفی می خواهد یک فرشته باشد؟
امّا فقط دختر ها فرشته هستند.“

The teacher stared. The teacher thought and said, "Alfie wants to be an angel? But only girls are angels."

آلفی به آرامی سرش را تکان داد،
و هر چه در بارهٔ فرشته ها می‌دانست به آموزگارش گفت.

Alfie slowly shook his head,
and he told his teacher all about the angels.

چطور آنها را در کتابهایش دیده است.
چطور آنها را در روهایش دیده است.

How he'd seen them in his books.
How he'd seen them in his dreams.

و هر چه آلفی بیشتر حرف زد، همهٔ کلاس بیشتر به حرفهایش گوش دادند.

And the more Alfie spoke,
the more the whole class listened.

هیچکس نخندید و هیچکس خندهٔ تمسخرآمیز سر نداد.
برای اینکه آلفی میخواست یک فرشته باشد.

Nobody laughed and nobody sniggered,
because Alfie wanted to be an angel.

Now it was that time of year when children could be angels.
The teachers taught them. The parents dressed them.
The whole school watched them while they sang and danced.

حالا آن وقت سال رسیده بود که بچه‌ها می‌توانستند فرشته شوند. آموزگاران به آنها یاد دادند. اولیاء آنها را لباس پوشاندند. تمام مدرسه رقص و آواز آنها را تماشا کردند.

آلفی یک فرشته بود!

Alfie was an angel!

15⁹⁵

OPENING YOUR EYES TO ART – 2

Identifying ART

By SHIRLEY HOCHMAN

STERLING PUBLISHING CO., INC.   NEW YORK

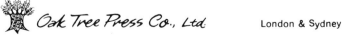
Oak Tree Press Co., Ltd.   London & Sydney

OTHER BOOKS OF INTEREST

Copyright © 1974 by Sterling Publishing Co., Inc.
419 Park Avenue South, New York, N.Y. 10016
British edition published by Oak Tree Press Co., Ltd., Nassau, Bahamas
Distributed in Australia and New Zealand by Oak Tree Press Co., Ltd.,
P.O. Box J34, Brickfield Hill, Sydney 2000, N.S.W.
Distributed in the United Kingdom and elsewhere in the British Commonwealth
by Ward Lock Ltd., 116 Baker Street, London W 1
Manufactured in the United States of America
All rights reserved
Library of Congress Catalog Card No.: 73-93594
Sterling ISBN 0-8069-5294-6 Trade   Oak Tree 7061-2483-9
5295-4 Library

Contents

Rembrandt van Rijn

"REMBRANDT AND SASKIA"

What Is Art?

Did you ever pick up a rock and admire its shape, color, and texture? Do you enjoy looking at a shell or examining the structure of a leaf? Do you think of the rock or the leaf as works of art? Or do you feel that an art object must be *made* for the purposes of art?

Once you have made up your mind what you think art is, you have the problem of deciding what is "good" art and what is "bad" art. This decision is entirely up to you. What *you* see and feel are important, and you can never be "wrong" when you express your honest feelings about a work of art.

The enjoyment of art is one of the great experiences in life. Men and women have never stopped creating ideas and images in paint, both for their own satisfaction and for other people's pleasure. So art has survived. Today, more people can view the world's masterpieces than ever before. When we are not able to see the original art, we can view printed reproductions. Illustrated books provide us with an instantly available "art gallery" which we can visit again and again.

Browse through this book as you would an art gallery. Looking at pictures is a way to begin, but look more than once. Soon the paintings will become familiar. You will discover ideas and images that you did not see at first glance. Let your imagination take over.

Then read about the paintings and the artists. The ideas presented may help you to find out how *you* feel about art. Remember, the worthwhile facts about art are those you discover for yourself.

This is the second volume in the series, "Open Your Eyes to Art." However, you may begin with this volume, which identifies some of the great periods of art. You may then go back and read the first volume, "Invitation to Art," which suggests ways to explore your ideas and feelings about art.

Art and History

The art of any period of history shows us how people lived and what they felt at the time. It reflects the ideals and values of the society that produced it. In these pages, we will look at art and find clues to the history of particular times and places. "The Night Watch," painted by Rembrandt van Rijn in 1642, for example, was a portrait of a military company. (See page 14.) Today, if a group of military men had a photograph taken, they would surely present a different picture. It is interesting to consider what the contrast might tell about our society, just the way "The Night Watch" tells about life during Rembrandt's time.

The Artist, the Time, and the Place

Artists, like everyone, mirror the times and the places they live in. Most people generally think and act very much like the people round them, but the artist is less worried about "what everyone else is doing." He or she must find a *personal* way of expressing feelings and ideas. Even so, the artist is affected by the things he sees and does, and *is* influenced by the people round him, but mostly by the work of other artists. No one is completely original. Artists often share ideas. They learn from each other and from artists of the past.

Art Periods

Artists of a particular period share an interest in similar subject matter, often work under similar conditions, and experiment with certain effects. As you become familiar with some of the major periods of art, you will begin to understand how art develops and flows in a continuous stream.

For example, Van Gogh might not have painted the bright, sun-filled "Harvest" shown on page 10 had he not first seen the work of Impressionist painters. Their sunny, out-of-doors views appealed to Van Gogh. His dark and gloomy paintings became filled with light.

Ideas about Art

At one time, no one would dream of a rocket to the moon. Later, only those with imagination and scientific knowledge could seriously consider the possibility. Today, flights to the moon are an accepted fact of life. In somewhat the same way, ideas in art begin as experiments, gain recognition, and, in time, become accepted by artists and the public.

Some experiments in art are short-lived. Most of them have little or no influence on the mainstream of art. Yet, sometimes rejected ideas are revived in some future time. The artist Georges de La Tour was rediscovered nearly three centuries after his death! (See page 20.)

Ideas about art continue to change. People agree and disagree. This exchange of ideas is part of the fun of art, and leads to lively discussions.

Be an Art Detective

The more you know of paintings, painters, and art periods, the more likely you are to become an art detective and be able to identify paintings. Make comparisons and contrasts between paintings. This will lead to encounters with art which enrich your life, and help you to find a meaningful and personal answer to the question, "What is art?"

The various art activities suggested in this book are for people who cannot draw. But, even if you are able to draw well, experimenting with the ideas and materials of art will help you to explore and develop your personal creativity. In addition, you will have fun. When your original work of art expresses your ideas and feelings, sign it proudly.

Try This

Gainsborough, an 18th-century English painter, liked to indulge his fancy or imagination. He arranged pebbles and twigs on a table top and painted the landscapes these miniatures suggested. These paintings were called "Gainsborough's fancies."

Try some "fancies" of your own. Arrange twigs, matches, pebbles, or crumbs to suggest a landscape. Pretend these small forms are mountains, valleys, huge rocks, and trees. Make a pencil sketch of your idea.

A
Breadcrumb
Moonscape

"RAIN, STEAM AND SPEED," Joseph Mallord William Turner.

ABOUT THE PAINTING

"Rain, Steam and Speed," Turner

1775–1851

"Rain, Steam and Speed" is one of Turner's most abstract (unrealistic) works. Painted in 1844, it was greeted with jeers by a public looking for solid realism and rejecting poetry in art. Today, the abstract quality of the images and the artist's poetic view of the ordinary are the things that mark this work as a masterpiece.

When this picture was painted, the steam locomotive was only 20 years old. The speed with which it roared across the countryside must have captured the imagination of that day in the same way as the fast cars, jets, and rockets of today fascinate us. However, the image of the train crossing the bridge at full speed is almost hidden, and the artist's delight in painting air and mist is obvious.

What did you first notice when you looked at this picture? How did Turner use color to make the train and the bridge stand out? If the train were painted in a light color, what would happen? Why did the artist use light colors next to dark colors? Have you ever looked at clouds in the sky and imagined you saw real things there? What can you see in the fog and mist of this painting? What things in this painting are made by Man? By Nature? Can you think of other names for this painting?

By the time Turner was 15 years old, his work was exhibited at the Royal Academy in London. Before he was 30, he became a Royal Academician. However, Turner cared little for this title, seldom met with other artists, and did little teaching at the Academy. Nevertheless, his work was recognized, and he was paid many commissions to paint for wealthy patrons.

As his earnings increased, the artist had enough money to travel. Wherever he went, there were new views to paint—fields, trees, hills, rivers, buildings, water, and boats. He worked hard to create on canvas and paper the elements of Nature—the sun, clouds, wind, water. People said that Turner was able to put the sun itself into his work! He also put into his paintings and drawings some of the brightness, joy, and spirit that were missing in his life.

In the early 1830's, Turner lost interest in painting the peaceful landscapes that had made him famous. He became fascinated with the furious, ever-changing and destructive moods of Nature. He painted great storms on land and sea with intense bursts of color. Peace was replaced by turbulence, movement, flames, fog, and storms. Turner painted as no one before had ever painted, and as might have been expected, he was rejected by the crowds who had previously admired his work. Their criticism deeply wounded the artist.

Gallery of Art, Leicester.

"THE GIUDECCA"

"STEAMER
IN
SNOWSTORM"

After Turner's death, his will revealed the true magnificence of his work. He left his greatest masterpieces to the people of England. There were about 19,000 drawings and paintings. He left his money to aid poor and aged artists. Turner's landscapes are among the treasures of 19th-century art. His most admired works show the formless beauty of air and water in a style that suggests the abstract art of the 20th century and the personal poetry of a timeless artist.

Try This

Receding Lines

Draw a horizontal line about one third of the distance between the top and the bottom of your paper. Sketch some lines to suggest tracks or a road receding to a vanishing point on the horizon. (Remember, distant things appear small.) Use pencil lines to create the effect of atmosphere. Consider rubbing these lines with your finger to achieve a soft effect.

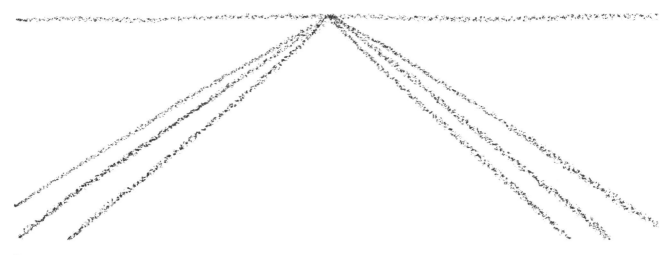

Try This

A Discovered Landscape

Dampen a piece of paper and crinkle it. Allow ink to drop on the surface of the paper. It will flow along the creased lines. When it is dry, flatten the paper and add lines to make the landscape you discover clear. The landscape may be the surface of a distant planet or a nearby country place.

ABOUT THE ARTIST

Joseph Mallord William Turner

1775–1851

Joseph Turner was the son of a poor London barber. He went from rags to riches as his fame as a painter grew, but his story does not follow a traditional pattern, and he did not live happily ever after. Turner lived a strange and secret life in which neither the rags nor the riches seemed to be important.

As a child, Turner loved to draw. He would sit in the barber shop drawing, and friends and customers began to admire his work. By the time he was 12 years old, he was able to sell his water colors for a few shillings. Turner worked at his art during the years that other children went to school, played, or learned a craft. In those days, the serious business of learning a trade began early for children of poor parents. Yet, in spite of hardship, Turner became successful very early in life.

Turner grew rich and famous, but his tastes were modest and his expenses small. During the years of success and fame, the artist sold only his second-best works. He hid the real masterpieces that came to light only after he died.

Turner eventually hid from everyone he knew, even living under a false name to be sure that no one would find him. He drank heavily, and finally became bedridden. As he lay dying, it is said that he asked to be taken to a window so that he could die gazing at the sunset. Turner never confided in anyone—all we know about him lies in his art.

ABOUT THE PAINTING

"The Harvest," Van Gogh

1853–1890

Colors had symbolic meanings for Van Gogh. For example, he once said, "How beautiful yellow is." He felt that yellow was the color of love and friendship, so he pictured fields "as far as one can see, green and yellow." In this painting, the wide fields of the French countryside gleam in the summer sun. It is a cloudless day, allowing us to see beyond the fields to the distant hills. The brilliant sky meets the horizon. This painting proves how right Van Gogh was about the beauty of yellow.

What kind of day did the artist picture? Did you ever visit or pass by a place like this? How many people can you find in the painting? How many farm carts? Houses and barns? Can you explain what the large group of buildings way off in the distance on the left is? Do you think it might be a centuries-old fort? Or a castle? What do you think is the most important part of the painting? Is it an object or is it a feeling that you get when you look at the painting? If it is a feeling, do you think it might be because of the colors the artist used?

What makes "The Harvest" great is that Van Gogh responded to the vitality of Nature. He gave an almost human energy to fields and trees. Notice how the scene is brought to life by the artist's short, quick, and rhythmic brush strokes. Can you see how the artist's hand must have moved? Can you trace the path of his loaded brush in the heavily textured paint? These short, visible brush strokes are Van Gogh's special "handwriting."

During his lifetime, Van Gogh tried to brighten the lives of people and often failed, but his paintings succeeded. He would sit out-

Tate Gallery, London.

"LANDSCAPE WITH CYPRESSES NEAR ARLES"

of-doors gazing at the beauty of Nature, intent on capturing sunlight on canvas. He pictured a great variety of subjects—cypress trees, sunflowers, simple interiors, fields, streets, and people.

The people that Van Gogh pictured were beautiful in spirit. Like Rembrandt, who lived 250 years before him, he was not

Louvre, Paris.

"THE ARTIST'S ROOM IN ARLES"

attracted by people's physical beauty. His portraits were of people with honest and upright character. Also like Rembrandt, Van Gogh painted many portraits of himself, using a mirror. In these self-portraits, Van Gogh was searching for his own identity. "What am I really like?" was the question he kept asking himself.

In his early work, Van Gogh pictured poor miners in Belgium where he did missionary work. (See "Potato Eaters.") Even in these dark and sometimes clumsy works, he showed the intensity of his feelings. Art did not come easily to him, however, and his lack of technical skill made Van Gogh search for, and eventually discover, an intensely personal style. He found a way to express the love for mankind that he felt deeply. These feelings, which Van Gogh could not express in his relationships with people, he expressed in his drawings and paintings.

Van Gogh's paintings are today treasured in the world's great museums and private collections and—what probably would have pleased Van Gogh even more—reproductions of his work brighten many simple homes.

"SELF PORTRAIT"

Try This

Use yellow, red, and orange crayons to create a sun. Try to apply small, strong strokes of color. Place one color next to the other to get a bright, sunny effect. Have the strokes of color go round and round to follow the shape of the whirling sun.

"THE POTATO EATERS"

Collection, The Museum of Modern Art, New York.   Gift of Mr. and Mrs. A. A. Rosen.

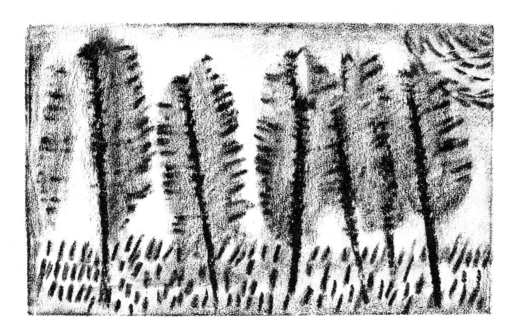

Try This

Create a Forest

Cut a small sprig of evergreen, an interesting weed, or other plant. A cutting of 2 or 3 inches (5 to 8 cm.) will not hurt the plant. Strip the foliage from the bottom third of the piece you have selected.

Place the foliage under a piece of paper. Now, use the flat side of a dark crayon to rub over the foliage. Rub firmly until you have an image, or "rubbing," on the paper. Now transfer the foliage to a different part of the paper. Have the rubbings overlap in some places. Space the rubbings to suggest a forest. You may add small strokes of broken color to suggest grass, haystacks, shrubs, or other objects. Sometimes, imagination takes over and such a "forest" becomes an unusual place.

You can make rubbings of small images cut from magazines and laid on another piece of paper or large images such as man-hole covers or any other raised surface.

ABOUT THE ARTIST

Vincent van Gogh. 1853–1890

Van Gogh was born in The Netherlands. All of his life he tried to help people. This urge caused him to go to Belgium as a young man to work among the poor miners of the Borinage area. Yet, in spite of high motives and unselfish service, Van Gogh's mission was a failure. He gave all he had to the poor and soon found himself in as bad a state as those he had come to help. The church that had sent him to help the poor dismissed him.

During these dark days, Vincent's brother Theo was his only friend. The artist would write long, emotion-filled letters to his brother. In one of these letters, Van Gogh explained his intention to devote all his time to art. Were it not for Theo's financial help and belief in Vincent's ability he might have starved.

Van Gogh's personal life was always unhappy. He felt hated and defeated. Yet, he also had an idea of his greatness. He wrote, "There is in me harmony, calm, and music." There was also conflict, anxiety, and discord.

While Vincent's work reflected his humanity and ideals, his personal relationships reflected the inner troubles that were to destroy him. When he was 35 years old, he cut off his own ear in a state of rage at himself. Later, at his own request, Van Gogh was admitted to a mental hospital. At this time he alternated between sanity and madness. During his well periods, he painted some of his greatest works.

When Van Gogh was only 37 years old, the struggle became unbearable to him, and he shot and killed himself.

Painted in about 1642. 12 ft. 2 in. × 14 ft. 7 in. (3.5 m. 5 cm. × 4 m. 18 cm.). Oil on Canvas. Rijksmuseum, Amsterdam, Holland.

"The Night Watch," Rembrandt

1601–1669

This large painting is a portrait of the civic guard of Amsterdam, Holland. Each man in the picture paid an equal amount of money to be included in the portrait. Group portraits were popular in 1642, when this picture was painted, for the camera had not yet been invented. While more ordinary artists might have lined up the guardsmen and given equal space to each member of the company, Rembrandt had other ideas. He was interested in creating a canvas showing activity and energy. So, he posed each figure to get the effect of movement in the total composition.

However, the men who had paid the artist to be in this portrait were not pleased with his work. They had wanted a picture that would clearly show the face of each member of the group, such as in "Syndics of the Cloth Hall."

What do you notice about the size of the important figures in "The Night Watch"? Do you think they are really the most important men in the group? Can you find the man whose face is hidden by the outstretched arm of his comrade? How do you think he might have felt about the way he was portrayed? Can you find other men who might have been unhappy about their position in the painting?

Notice the beautiful golden tones for which this artist is famous. Can you see how he used light to direct attention to the two officers leading the group? Can you find other areas of the painting where Rembrandt used light in this way? This work was first named "The Company of Captain Frans Banning Cocq." Later, it was called "The Night Watch" because it appeared to be a night scene. However, when the work was cleaned in 1946, the mid-afternoon sun could be seen streaming into the dark assembly hall, where the officers had gathered before a shooting match. Still, the title, "The Night Watch," has remained.

It is said that Rembrandt lost his popularity as a portrait painter because of "The

"SYNDICS OF THE CLOTH HALL"

"DAVID AND SAUL"

Mauritshuis, The Hague.

Notice how both artists were concerned with the effect of light. Both men made images of real people captured at a special moment, and both call the viewers' attention to the focal point of interest in a painting by directional lines, colors, and effects of light.

When wealthy people no longer came to him for portraits, and he went hungry, Rembrandt found friends in the Amsterdam ghetto. He continued to work and showed no sign of defeat or discouragement. He showed only great sympathy for other people. Living in poverty, Rembrandt painted some of his greatest works. He pictured Man and his condition in paintings that searched men's souls.

Night Watch." People were afraid to have Rembrandt paint their portraits. They wanted safe, familiar poses and above all they wanted to be seen.

Rembrandt enjoyed doing paintings in his own way, never merely to please a sitter. He pictured old people, the poor, and members of his family. He pictured characters and stories from the Old Testament. For models, he sought out elderly Jews and dressed them in rich costumes. He found in their faces strong human emotions. In painting this way, Rembrandt felt free to express his inner visions and convictions. At the same time, he developed an elegant, original, and masterly style. He had an ability to suggest details with a skilful stroke of his brush. His paintings gleamed in a golden light that contrasted with his rich, dark colors. Figures came to life in natural poses that revealed character.

It is interesting to compare Rembrandt's elaborate masterpiece, "The Night Watch," with La Tour's "Newborn Babe." (See page 18.) Both works were done about the same time. Both painters were exposed to the same traditions, and were products of the same age. The contrast in styles illustrates the variety of the artists' expression. This personal quality, or "signature," is what distinguishes the work of one artist from that of another.

Try This

Costume a Character

Select a family photograph or a newspaper or magazine picture of a contemporary man or woman, and paste this face on a background paper. With paint or soft-tip pen, add details of costume and hair style. You might try the costumes of 17th-century Holland pictured in "The Night Watch." Besides being fun, this experiment might suggest the heritage we share with the past.

16

Try This

Do a Group Portrait

A group portrait may be solid and serious or imaginative and amusing. Cut out people from copies of class photographs, magazines, and so on. Arrange these images in a group portrait. You may overlap figures, give them unusual poses, or make them appear in fantastic relationships. Consider using paint or crayons to add details and to bring the separate images into a closer relationship.

ABOUT THE ARTIST

Rembrandt van Rijn. 1601–1669

Rembrandt's father owned a windmill in Holland. Although the miller wanted his son to be a lawyer, young Rembrandt's remarkable talent soon made it clear that he was to be an artist. After some formal study, the artist set himself up in the business of painting portraits. The prosperous Dutch were attracted by the quality of Rembrandt's work, and soon the artist had many portrait commissions.

These were his happiest days. He married Saskia and found joy in his family and work. He lived in a large and expensive house and collected jewelry, paintings, and precious objects. Some say that his extravagance in these days contributed to his later downfall. Then, his beloved Saskia died at the age of 30. At that time, Rembrandt was working on "The Night Watch." Saddened by Saskia's death and by the reaction to his painting, he began to care less and less about the opinion of others. His popularity declined, but he was left free to draw and paint subjects of his own choice. He declared this freedom to be the only thing worthwhile in life.

In time, Rembrandt remarried. His domestic life was peaceful, but he allowed his financial affairs to go from bad to worse. Rembrandt had to give up his possessions to pay his debts, and his great art collection was sold for a fraction of its value. He died in Amsterdam, alone and poor.

"SELF PORTRAIT"

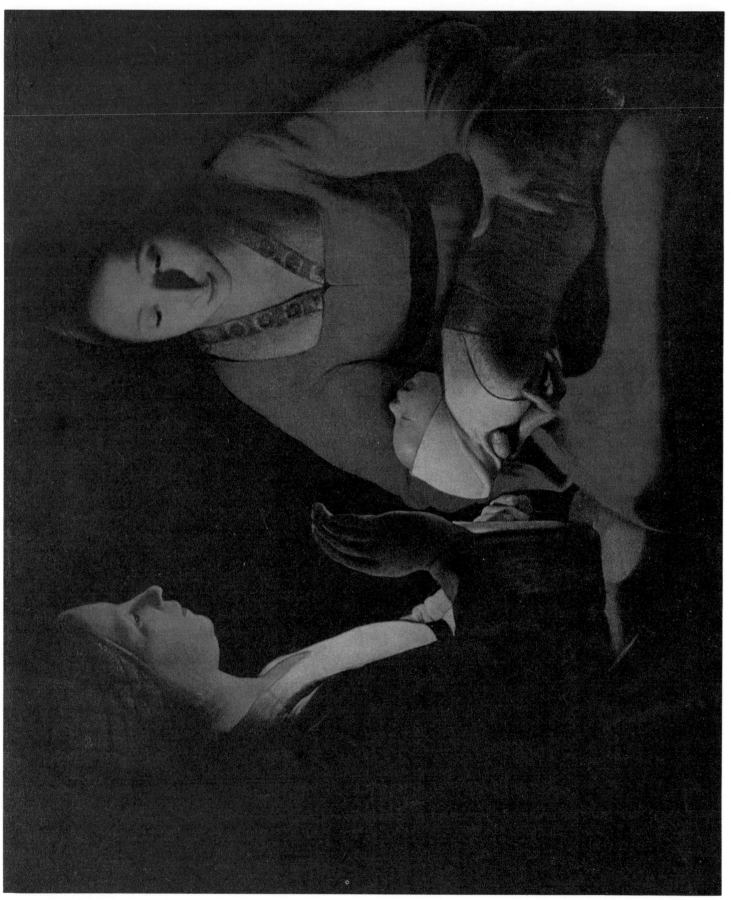

Painted in about 1640. 30 × 35¾ in. (76 × 91 cm.). Oil on Canvas. Museum of Rennes, Rennes, France.

"Newborn Babe," La Tour

1593–1652

When this picture was painted, it was the custom to wrap infants with bands of cloth called "swaddling clothes." It was thought that these tight wrappings kept infants safe and healthy. Here, a mother tenderly holds her newborn child while another woman admires the infant by the light of a candle. La Tour communicates the dignity and inner beauty of the women, a beauty that goes beyond mere prettiness. We can actually feel their love for the infant. An air of wonder and religious mystery fills the canvas in this deeply serious painting.

What feelings do *you* get from this painting? How does the artist use light? Is it used in the same way as in Rembrandt's "The Night Watch"? (See page 14.) Do the simple shapes that La Tour uses appeal to you? Notice that the figures of the women form two triangles. These large shapes in contrasting dark and light colors seem to make the candlelight shine brightly and impart a special glow to the painting.

Louvre, Paris.

"ST. JOSEPH THE CARPENTER"

Even though this painting is over 300 years old, do you feel that it has a "timeless" quality? That its simplicity is similar to many modern paintings? For example, can you find any similarity between "Newborn Babe" and "The Dressmakers," which was painted 250 years later? (See page 34.)

Louvre, Paris.

"THE REPENTANT MAGDALENE"

These paintings illustrate the deep, dark shadows typical of La Tour's art.

A church, Broglie (Eure).

"ST. SEBASTIAN HEALED BY ST. IRENE"

19

Louvre, Paris.

"ADORATION
OF THE
SHEPHERDS"

La Tour's greatest ability was in painting the night. In "Newborn Babe" notice how the darkness of night is created by the use of light from a single source—the candle. Through this special glow, for which the artist is famous, he was able to picture everyday scenes in a spiritual light, such as in "St. Joseph the Carpenter." In that painting also, the light suggests a divine presence and takes on a deeply religious meaning. All of La Tour's paintings were based on his own religious faith and daily life.

The beauty of La Tour's art was only discovered in 1915, close to three centuries after the painter died. Today, when we look at the simple outlines of his figures, the dramatic effects of soft glowing light, and the poetic quality of his work, we wonder how his work could have gone unnoticed for so long.

ABOUT THE ARTIST

Georges de La Tour. 1593–1652

Not a great deal is known about the life of this artist. He lived in Nancy, France, which was then a small town. The townspeople admired his work, but people beyond Nancy knew nothing of his tender and deeply religious paintings. Then, in 1633, the King of France came to live in Nancy to escape a terrible plague which had struck Paris.

The King wanted an artist to paint a special religious painting, and that is how he discovered La Tour. By chance, the obscure country painter became artist to the King. But the royal patronage did not last long. The King returned to Paris when the threat of the plague was over, and La Tour was forgotten.

Until the early 20th century, La Tour's work was thought to be that of other artists, such as Jan Vermeer of Holland and Louis Le Nain of France. When his paintings were finally identified by experts in 1915, he was "rediscovered." Since then his fame has been increasing steadily among people who love art, and his simple and inspiring works are treasured by the museums and collectors who own them.

Try This

Sketching Shadows

Place a few simple objects on a table. Try fruits, shells, or any objects that attract you, but start with objects that have simple outlines. Now, do not sketch the objects themselves; instead, sketch the light and dark areas that surround them. When the background shapes make the outlines of the objects clear, consider adding tones to the objects.

You can also experiment with light and dark by creating shapes that do not refer to real things. Use a pencil, black crayon or charcoal. Create dark, deep areas that contrast with light areas. The dark and light areas can be in sharp contrast or they might be softly blended.

Try This

"The Golden Triangle"

The artist Leonardo da Vinci used the triangle as a basic form in many of his masterpieces. Notice this basic form in the "Mona Lisa." La Tour's figures in "Newborn Babe" also fit into triangles. Sketch a triangle and fit the head and shoulders of a figure into this space.

Louvre, Paris.

"MONA LISA," Leonardo da Vinci.

"Storm in the Jungle," Rousseau

1844–1910

In this painting, we see a jungle of the artist's imagination. A strong wind moves branches and leaves and distant lightning appears in the sky. Notice that even in the fury of the storm, Rousseau pictured each leaf distinctly and in place. Note the clear outlines of each shape. Rousseau was attempting to paint an exact and realistic image. However, the charm of his work lies in the manner in which he changes reality, and creates a personal "fairy tale." Here, he did not merely picture a storm, he *created* one.

When you first looked at this painting, did you feel the storm? How does the artist show the feeling of movement that accompanies a storm? How did he paint the rain? The grass? What is your feeling about the tiger? Do you think he is running from the storm or do you think he is about to pounce on a prey? Does he look frightened or frightening? What color struck you when you first looked at the painting? Was it the different shades of green? Or the splotches of red here and there? Compare the way in which Rousseau painted rain and movement with "Rain, Steam and Speed" by Turner. (See page 6.) How are they alike? In what ways are they different?

Rousseau had a fine sense of color. Notice the great variety of greens and yellows. The contrast of light shades of color next to dark shades makes each part of the painting stand out clearly. The patches of bright red add excitement to the painting. The variety of shapes and colors are typical of Rousseau's imaginative approach to creating art.

Rousseau was a "Sunday painter." Born in France, he visited Mexico as an enlisted

"THE SNAKE-CHARMER"

Musée du Jeu de Paume, Paris.

ABOUT THE ARTIST

Henri Rousseau. 1844–1910

Rousseau was born in Laval, in northwestern France, the son of a tinsmith. After serving in the French Army, he got a job collecting customs duties in Paris when he was 35 years old. During this time, he began to paint as a hobby. Five years later, Rousseau decided to quit his job and devote all of his time to art. Few people would have guessed that the customs collector would become a successful and famous artist.

Rousseau had great ambition but no formal training in art, so he taught himself. While he was poor, he could not sell his work or even exchange it for the things he needed. Unknowing people thought his work had no value.

Years later, when Rousseau's status as an artist was recognized, art collectors and dealers visited the places where he had lived as a customs officer, trying to find overlooked examples of his art. One old friend recalled having once owned paintings by Rousseau and said, "Why, we threw them out long ago!" This was certainly a foolish and costly mistake.

Rousseau's paintings were praised by some of the great and famous artists of his own day. In 1906, Pablo Picasso recognized Rousseau's work and gave a dinner for him. A famous poet called Rousseau's art "painted poetry." In time, the public came to appreciate Rousseau's honesty, simplicity, and charm. Today, Rousseau has become one of the best known and highly prized of the self-taught painters.

man in the army. The images of Mexico—birds, plants, tropical forests, and animals made a deep impression on Rousseau, and it came out in his art 20 years later. But the most important sources for the animals and plants that he loved to picture were the zoos and botanical gardens of Paris. He transformed his memories and observations into exotic scenes of jungles and animals.

Rousseau's jungles are always arranged in formal decorative patterns. Each form is

"VASE OF FLOWERS"

"THE
SLEEPING
GYPSY"

Collection, The Museum of Modern Art.
Gift of Mrs. Simon Guggenheim.

24

"PORTRAIT OF JOSEPH
BRUNNER"

technique are usually self-taught, or "primitive," and Rousseau did teach himself to paint.

Try This

Draw a Jungle Vine

Use a black crayon to draw a twisting vine, using a curved line. Draw a leaf on a separate paper and cut out this leaf. Place the leaf *under* the drawing paper, arrange it somewhere along the vine, and rub over the top side of the paper with the long side of a dark crayon. Work directly over the leaf, and the image, or "rubbing," of the leaf will appear. Then move the leaf to another position and repeat until the design satisfies you. Then make a variety of leaves, flowers, birds, or other objects to create a whole jungle scene.

clearly outlined. He created patterns with a natural sense of design and a sensitive understanding of color. Animals with almost human faces appear in his fairy-tale jungles. His work was not about the reality of a jungle, but his dream of what a jungle would be like. Artists who use this detailed and painstaking

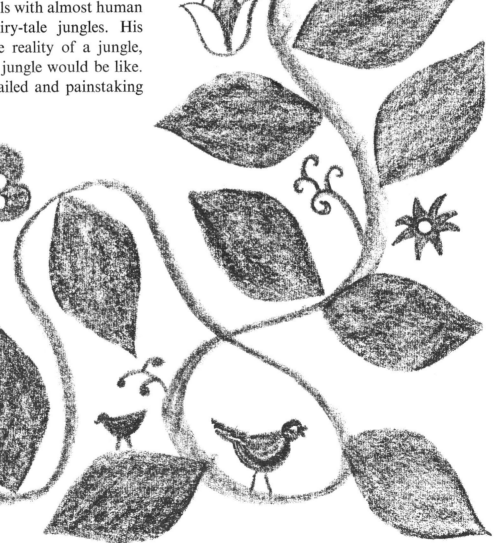

25

Painted in about 1830. 30 × 35⅞ in. (76 × 91 cm.). Oil on Canvas. National Gallery of Art, Washington, D.C. Collection of Edgar William and Bernice Chrysler Garbisch.

"Peaceable Kingdom," Hicks

1780–1849

Hicks painted over 60 versions of "Peaceable Kingdom"—it was the subject that he liked best. Each of the 60 was a different variation on the same theme. Here, wild beasts, farm animals and children are pictured in a quiet country place. All are living together in complete harmony. In the distance at the left, William Penn is concluding his famous treaty of peace with the Indians.

Each animal is clearly pictured in the very detailed and stiff style of the primitive, or self-taught, painter. The animals seem to be piled one on top of the other, and they are not always proportionate in size. It is the beauty of the arrangement, not its realism, that appeals to the viewer. Each animal has become part of the total design.

The painting, a celebration of peace, illustrates that happy day, predicted in the Bible in the Book of Isaiah, when "the lion shall lie down with the lamb."

How did you feel when you first looked at this painting? Were you surprised to see fierce and gentle animals side by side? The artist wanted to remind people of a day in the future when men will live at peace and

Painting by Thomas Hicks.

"EDWARD HICKS"

ABOUT THE ARTIST

Edward Hicks. 1780–1849

Edward Hicks, an American painter, was nine years old when George Washington became the first President of the United States. His family had lost all their money during the Revolutionary War. As a boy, Hicks was not a good student, but he loved studying the Bible and remembering all of the Biblical stories he heard at home. He also enjoyed making things with his hands, so it was decided that Edward should learn a trade.

At the age of 13, he was apprenticed to a coachmaker. When this training was completed, Hicks set up a shop where he repaired and painted coaches. He also painted shop signs,

street signs, and furniture. One day, after work, Hicks decided to paint a picture. From that day on, painting became part hobby and part business for him. He found he could fully express his ideas and feelings in painting and that people enjoyed his work, enabling him to sell paintings for a modest price.

In later years, after an unsuccessful attempt at farming, Edward Hicks wrote, "I quit the only business I understood and for which I had a capacity, namely painting, for the business of a farmer, which I did not understand and for which I had no qualifications whatever."

"Nation shall not lift sword against nation nor ever be trained for war." Do you think we are any closer to that day than when this painting was made almost 150 years ago? Do you think the subject of this painting is even more important for people to think about today?

As you look at the painting, which animals seem to be most important? Do you feel that each animal is just as important as all of the rest? How did the artist place the animals to make you feel this way? Do you think there is a special reason why Hicks chose to use so many different shades of brown? Do you think it was because the painting was made in Autumn? Or because he was trying to bring the animals closer to each other in every way possible?

Can you compare this painting in any way with Rembrandt's "The Night Watch"? (See page 14.) How did these two artists, Hicks and Rembrandt, differ in their feelings about placing the various figures in their paintings?

What was the important thing to Rembrandt? To Hicks? Do you think that there is any similarity in the use of color and light in the paintings? If so, do you feel that the artists had the same reasons for their use of color and light?

Edward Hicks was a Pennsylvania Quaker who followed the peaceful ways of Quakers and was active in Quaker affairs. Although he earned his living at a variety of different trades, he was well known as a Quaker minister, travelling about the countryside, visiting Quaker families and speaking at their meetings. It is a reflection of his beliefs that his most famous paintings are about a world at peace.

Try This
Your Own Peaceable Kingdom
From newspapers, magazines and photographs, select pictures of people, places, and pets in your life. Arrange these pictures in an original and modern version of the peaceable kingdom.

"THE
CORNELL
FARM"

National Gallery of Art, Washington D.C. Gift of Edgar William and Bernice Chrysler Garbisch.

Try This

A Collage about Peace

Collect newspaper and magazine pictures to create a collage about a world at peace. Select whatever scenes, people, or things you think symbolize peace. Arrange these images on a background paper so that they overlap or poke through openings or slits that you can make in the paper. The work need not be realistic. It should create a mood or express your ideas and ideals. Experiment with various arrangements before pasting any parts in place.

Try This

Create Wild Beasts

Scribble over a sheet of paper. Then, search your scribble for lines and shapes that suggest real or imaginary animals. Use color to make the images you discover in the scribble clear.

"RED HORSES," Franz Marc.

Painted in about 1911. 47¼ × 71⅛ in. (120 × 181 cm.). Oil on Canvas. Private Collection, Rome.

ABOUT THE PAINTING

"Red Horses," Marc

1880–1916

This artist was fascinated by the animal world and particularly by horses. He realized that we all know how a horse looks, but in this painting he wanted to demonstrate the strength, power, and intelligence of horses. The color red suggests courage, so Marc uses red here to force us to take a new look at the horses after our attention is attracted by the unusual color.

Marc is able to point up the graceful and rhythmic movements of these large animals by repeating the flowing curves of their necks and bodies in the curves of the landscape. Also, he uses the same symbolic colors to describe both landscape and horses. In this way, he shows how animals and Nature exist in harmony in this imaginary world of color.

The horses are apart from humans and exist on their own terms. They are not gentle beasts to be trained and broken, but animals viewed in their private world.

How do these horses seem to you? Happy? Worried? Watchful? How does this artist's unusual use of colors affect you? Have you ever seen a yellow sky? Blue trees and rocks? Red grass? Do you feel that the artist has the right to use these imaginary colors?

How do these animals compare with those in "Peaceable Kingdom"? (See page 26.) Do you like carefully painted animals with each detail showing? Or do you prefer soft and suggested shapes? How does this landscape compare with that in "Peaceable Kingdom"? How does it compare with Van Gogh's "The Harvest"? (See page 10.)

In his work, Marc pictured a whole world

"WHITE BULL"

The Solomon R. Guggenheim Museum, New York.

"YELLOW COW"

The Solomon R. Guggenheim Museum, New York.

in imaginary colors. He said, "I should like meadows colored red and trees colored blue." He searched for his models in zoos and fields. Then he tried to imagine the world as it would appear to a horse or a cow. For example, one of his paintings was called, "This Is How My Dog Sees the World."

Notice how the artist keeps repeating freely brushed bright colors. The yellows and greens of the background make the sharpest possible contrast to the reds. These colors also suggest bright, open spaces. The artist is loudly proclaiming in this painting his freedom to select the colors he finds expressive, rather than the colors that mirror reality.

ABOUT THE ARTIST

Franz Marc was born in Munich, Germany. When he was 20 years old, he decided to become an artist and he went to art school. In these early years, his colors were naturalistic. He pictured things as they were, and his images were true to the models he observed.

In time, Marc visited Paris and saw the experimental art of other artists of the early 20th century, some of them "Expressionists." Observing that color could be used to express emotions, he decided to try it and paint in a new way. As Marc became aware of the artistic freedom that marks the art of the 20th century, he began to change reality to express his inner visions, his ideas, and his feelings. The increasingly abstract work of the artist Kandinsky held a special appeal for Franz Marc.

Marc's colors became more and more

Franz Marc

1880–1916

intense, and his shapes more and more abstract. He tried to express the essence, rather than the outward appearance, of his subjects, such as the horses shown in "Stables." In 1911, Marc became the leader of *Der Blaue Reiter* (The Blue Rider), a group of experimental artists. They took their name from the title of a painting by Kandinsky.

Franz Marc's promising career ended with World War I. The artist was killed in action at the age of 36.

"STABLES"

Try This

Think about the scenes that very young children picture in their drawings, such as houses, trees, flowers, and birds. Remember, most children's drawings have a sun shining somewhere.

Make a drawing, adding your own ideas to the world that children picture. Use bright, unusual colors to express your feelings about the scene.

Try This

The artist, Franz Marc, tried to imagine the world as it looked to animals. Try to imagine what you must look like to a small insect. Imagine that it is crawling over your finger, face, or sleeve. An insect might explore your face as you would explore a mountain. Make a drawing of some part of yourself showing a tiny creature and how you think you seem to him.

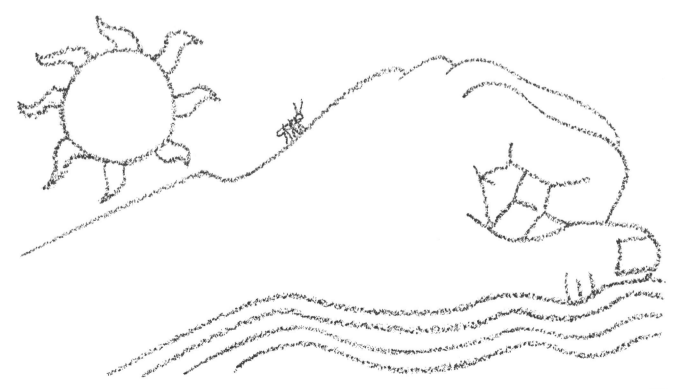

Painted in about 1891. 21 × 18 in. (53 × 46 cm.). Oil on Canvas. From the Collection of Doris Warner Vidor.

"The Dressmakers," Vuillard

1868–1940

In this painting, the artist Vuillard expressed the intimacy of people at work without making a photographic picture. The skill and competence with which the women work is reflected in the gentle curves of fabric and the quiet figures.

The artist reduced the shapes to flat designs that depict the subject. Notice the simplicity and variety of these shapes, which can be viewed as a design apart from the subject. The bright reds and greens take on a jewel-like brilliance through contrast with the black and brown areas.

Do you think there is a reason why the clothing worn by the dressmakers themselves is so drab? Compare it with the rich, red fabric they are working on. Do you think the artist might be hinting at the great separation between the world of fashion and the world of work? Do you think these two women are happy and enjoying what they are doing? If so, what has the artist done to make you feel that way? Do you think that the artist is expressing a feeling of sympathy and affection for the dressmakers?

Vuillard's painting invites us to visit the

"THE VISIT"

National Gallery of Art, Washington, D.C. Chester Dale Collection.

"VICTOR DURET"

his mother and sister who were dressmakers. He must have often watched them at their daily tasks.

"The Dressmakers" is typical of this artist's paintings in that he always pictured the charm and beauty in ordinary things and everyday pursuits. Vuillard led a quiet life and his art was very much like him—sensitive and peaceful. He pictured interiors of middle-class houses and delighted in showing the patterns that decorated walls and furnishings. This can be seen in both the paintings, "Victor Duret" and "The Visit."

Vuillard's paintings all show happy people at home in their natural environment. Does this remind you of the way in which Franz Marc pictured animals? (See page 31.) Do Marc's animals appear happy and content in their own world? Do they seem apart from anything that might be going on outside their immediate environment? Both artists used bright reds and greens. Do you think they had the same reasons for doing so?

dressmakers and share the contentment they find in their work. Perhaps the artist pictured

ABOUT THE ARTIST

Edouard Vuillard. 1868–1940

This painter was born in Cuiseaux, France. When he was nine years old, his family moved to Paris. His father died when Edouard was 15, and his mother opened a dressmaking shop to support her three children. Vuillard's paintings are often about his family and the working-class people who were their friends. The artist never travelled; he found his inspiration in his own surroundings.

After studying at some of the finest art schools in Paris, Vuillard dedicated his life to art. Among his friends were many of the famous artists of his day. Unlike the adventurous and dashing artist that we often picture in our imagination, Vuillard led a simple life. If he did not experience high adventure, he at least found contentment.

In an aggressive age, when artists vied for public attention with new theories, wild activities, and eccentric art, Vuillard stands out for his simple outlook on life.

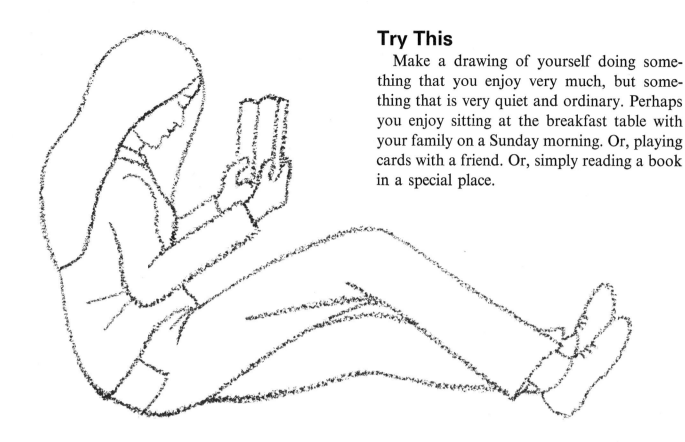

Try This

Make a drawing of yourself doing something that you enjoy very much, but something that is very quiet and ordinary. Perhaps you enjoy sitting at the breakfast table with your family on a Sunday morning. Or, playing cards with a friend. Or, simply reading a book in a special place.

Try This

The artist Vuillard enjoyed painting the many patterns he saw all round him. Look for interesting patterns in your own home, school, or in your friends' clothing. Then create a pattern of your own, using lines and other shapes. Remember, a pattern is simply a repeating of one thing in an orderly fashion.

Try This

Select either paints, crayons or pastels, and create a design of curved shapes in bright contrasting colors. The curved shapes might suggest a landscape or simply be an abstract design.

Art Movements

The Baroque Period

Rembrandt van Rijn, one of the great artists of all time, was a master of the 17th-century Baroque Period. This was the "golden age" of Dutch painting. The Baroque artist created an illusion of three dimensions on the flat canvas. Light, glowing colors contrasted with dark, rich colors and suggested rounded, realistic forms. Figures were pictured in dramatic, action-filled poses.

Artists were interested in showing elegant costumes, ornaments and shimmering textures. They developed great technical skill in painting. The subjects of the Dutch paintings of this period reflect the liberal, middle-class society of 17th-century Holland. The Dutch liked pictures of food, portraits of merchants, and peaceful landscapes, and artists were free to develop independent styles.

The term "Baroque" originally ridiculed this style which was considered distorted and lacking in classical beauty, overly decorative and sensational, and not refined in character. Baroque art was attacked for its break with tradition just as modern art movements of the 20th century are attacked for their break with realism.

Georges de La Tour was a French artist of the Baroque Period. Although most artists of the period were concerned with elaborate design, movement, and softly blended colors, La Tour was interested in simplified forms and limited colors. Only the subject matter of his paintings was in the Baroque tradition.

The Romantic Period

Joseph Turner lived during the Romantic Period that developed in 18th- and early 19th-century England. Romantic artists were individualists. They cast aside old formal orders and went to Nature for inspiration.

Turner's paintings reflect the Romantic taste for stormy, sweeping and violent aspects of Nature. Romantic art often tells a story and presents dramatic events. The arrival of the steam locomotive symbolized the Industrial Revolution of the 19th century. It was still a dramatic event when Turner painted, "Rain, Steam and Speed."

Turner was one of the first landscape artists to make sketches out-of-doors. It is sometimes said that he was the first Impressionist. His interest in the effects of air and light relate to the Impressionists. But Turner's subject matter was true to the Romantic school. Turner painted storms and shipwrecks, while the Impressionists painted sunlit fields and happy people.

The originality of Turner's art, the abstract quality of his work, his roots in the Romantic tradition, and his relationship to the art of the Impressionists—all ensure Turner's place in the history of art.

Impressionism

Impressionism was an important art movement of the 19th century. The Impressionists rejected the dark colors, dramatic stories, and posed pictures painted by the artists who came before them. They used light and bright colors, everyday subjects, and they often painted out-of-doors. By placing small strokes of broken color side by side, they achieved the blends they wanted.

Vincent van Gogh painted dark and serious pictures until he visited Paris and saw the work of the Impressionists. His eyes were opened to bright colors and a happy view of life. However, Van Gogh was not concerned with just the effects of light. Rather, he expressed deep feelings about people and places. Even his landscapes pictured Nature as though trees, grass, stars, and flowers had an almost human vitality. Because of this emotional, expressive quality, Van Gogh stands out among the Impressionists of his time.

In the same way that Turner anticipated the Impressionists with his interest in atmospheric effects, Van Gogh, with his interest in expressing feelings and emotions, foresaw an art movement of the 20th century—Expressionism.

Experimental Art

What is called modern art began in the 20th century. It breaks with the traditions of the past and the artist is free to experiment and find materials as well as methods that will express what he feels along with what he sees.

Experiments in art are not new. The Impressionists experimented with the changing effects of light. Later came the Expressionists, such as Franz Marc, with new ways to picture man's feelings, responses, and rebellions.

Other artists searched for ways to express man and his environment in terms of the cylinder, the cube, the sphere, and the cone. They felt that geometric forms could be used to express the form and content of experience. This group of artists were called Cubists.

Experiments in art have continued through Expressionism and Cubism into many current movements.

Primitive Art

A primitive artist searches for a way to express reality, a reality based on a personal vision of how things are, how things were, or how things should be. The self-taught, primitive painter may illustrate scenes from daily life or images drawn from fantasy and imagination.

Primitives paint for their own pleasure.

They take great pains to be exact and often fill their pictures with brightly colored details. They paint in a stiff and formal manner that, at times, suggests the simplified shapes of abstract art. However, the primitive artist does not intend to create abstract images as he is deeply tied to realism as the goal, but not the result, of his efforts.

Henri Rousseau was called "the father of primitives." Like all primitives, he was not influenced by the art of his time. Although he lived among the Impressionists, he paid little attention to their theories. He illustrates the complete sincerity and direct approach to painting that mark the work of the primitive artist.

In the late 18th century and throughout the 19th century, the self-taught, or primitive, artist flourished in New England. Many New Englanders lived on farms or in isolated communities, with little or no opportunity to view art or receive formal instruction. Under these conditions, the self-taught artists developed a uniquely American style.

They painted still-life arrangements, landscapes, figures, and portraits that reflect the simplicity of their lives. Many of these artists did not sign their paintings and they remain anonymous. Among those we can identify, the name of Edward Hicks stands out.

Today, the art of the true primitive is increasingly valued. But we live in an age of instant communication that makes it difficult to approach any activity with the fresh, original vision of a primitive. Perhaps a longing for a simpler, more honest way of life makes the art of primitives so appealing today.

Great art does not always fit exactly into one trend or style. Its originality is the mark of its greatness. However, as you continue to identify artists and periods of art, you will discover that artists, like all people, are influenced by the past and the era in which they live. In turn, they influence the future.

Index